SIMON SPOTLIGHT

An imprint of Simon & Schuster Children's Publishing Division

1230 Avenue of the Americas, New York, New York 10020

This Simon Spotlight edition December 2017

Snoopy Takes Off! adapted by Tina Gallo; illustrated by Scott Jeralds
© 2015 Peanuts Worldwide LLC

Go Fly a Kite, Charlie Brown! adapted by Cordelia Evans; illustrated by Will Yak
© 2015 Peanuts Worldwide LLC

Lose the Blanket, Linus! adapted by Tina Gallo; illustrated by Robert Pope
© 2015 Peanuts Worldwide LLC

It's Hockey Time, Franklin! adapted by Jason Cooper; illustrated by Scott Jeralds
© 2017 Peanuts Worldwide LLC

Cool Like Snoopy adapted by Daphne Pendergrass; illustrated by Vicki Scott
© 2016 Peanuts Worldwide LLC

Messy Like Pigpen adapted by Natalie Shaw; illustrated by Vicki Scott
© 2016 Peanuts Worldwide LLC

Sweet Like Sally adapted by R. J. Cregg; illustrated by Vicki Scott
© 2016 Peanuts Worldwide LLC

Snoopy for President! adapted by Maggie Testa; illustrated by Scott Jeralds
© 2016 Peanuts Worldwide LLC

Kick the Football, Charlie Brown! adapted by Cordelia Evans; illustrated by Scott Jeralds
© 2016 Peanuts Worldwide LLC

A Best Friend for Snoopy Based on the characters created by Charles M. Schulz
by Cala Spinner; illustrated by Scott Jeralds © 2016 Peanuts Worldwide LLC

A Best Friend for Woodstock Based on the characters created by Charles M. Schulz
by Tina Gallo; illustrated by Scott Jeralds © 2016 Peanuts Worldwide LLC

Snoopy and Woodstock's Great Adventure adapted by Lauren Forte; illustrated by Scott Jeralds
© 2015 Peanuts Worldwide LLC

For information about special discounts for bulk purchases, please contact Simon & Schuster Special Sales at 1-866-506-1949 or business@simonandschuster.com.

Manufactured in China 0518 SCP

10 9 8 7 6 5 4 3 2

ISBN 978-1-5344-1162-3

ISBN 978-1-5344-1169-2 (eBook)

These titles were previously published individually by Simon Spotlight with slightly different text and art.

Contents

Snoopy Takes Off!

This is Snoopy. He may look like a regular dog to you, but in fact, he is anything but ordinary!

Snoopy doesn't do anything the same way as an ordinary dog, starting with the way he sleeps *on* his doghouse, rather than inside.

It's a perfect day for me to jump in my plane, soar through the air, and fight the Red Baron! Snoopy thinks.

When Snoopy says he is going to "jump in his plane," he really means he's going to sit on top of his doghouse. He puts on his goggles, scarf, and helmet. "Here's the World War I Flying Ace flying across the sky in his Sopwith Camel airplane," Snoopy says. "Where are you, Red Baron?"

Suddenly Snoopy spots the Red Baron's plane! He is finally going to capture the enemy!

"Full speed ahead!" Snoopy shouts. But as fast as Snoopy is, the Red Baron is faster. He gets away . . . again. "Noooo!" Snoopy shouts. "Next time you are mine, Red Baron!"

Snoopy takes off his helmet and sits down. He turns around and sees Charlie Brown standing with his food dish.

"I wonder what it would be like to have a normal dog," Charlie Brown tells him.

Snoopy ignores him and concentrates on his food. Being a World War I Flying Ace works up an appetite!

Later that afternoon Snoopy is bored, so he decides to write the next Great American Novel. He pulls out his trusty old typewriter and begins to write.

It was a dark and stormy night.

Linus walks by and is curious.
Snoopy hands Linus the page.
"Your new novel has a very exciting beginning,"
Linus says.
Snoopy smiles proudly.
Linus hands back the sheet of paper. "Well, good
luck with the second sentence," he says.

Lucy is curious about Snoopy's book too. She has a suggestion for him. "You should begin your story with 'Once upon a time.' That's the way all good stories begin."

Snoopy thinks Lucy may be right, so he changes the beginning of his story. He types:

Once upon a time, it was a dark and stormy night.

Lucy looks at the new sheet of paper and groans. "Can't you write about something nice?" she asks Snoopy.

Snoopy thinks this is a good idea. So he types. Then he stops typing, and to Lucy's surprise, he jumps off his doghouse . . .

Once upon a time, it was a dark and stormy night. Suddenly, a kiss rang out!

. . . and he gives Lucy a big kiss!

"Aaagh, I've been kissed by a dog! I've got dog germs!" Lucy cries, and runs away.

That wasn't nearly as romantic as I thought it would be, Snoopy thinks.

Snoopy decides it's time for a dance break! There's nothing Snoopy loves more than dancing!

He dances with Charlie Brown!

He dances with Lucy!

He dances with Linus!

He even dances on top of Schroeder's piano! (Schroeder doesn't like this very much.)

After all that dancing, it's time for a snack.
Snoopy invites his best friend, Woodstock, to come
over. Even though Snoopy enjoys the dog food
Charlie Brown brings him, he is also a fabulous cook,
and loves whipping up surprises for his friends.

Woodstock loves hanging out with Snoopy, and tells him all about his day. Fortunately for Woodstock, Snoopy is fluent in bird, and understands every word he says.

Woodstock wants to go on a camping trip with Snoopy and some of his friends.

"Follow me, troops," Snoopy says. "And I don't want to see anyone hanging around my feet!"

The birds are very nervous about the hike. They want to stay as close to Snoopy as possible, so they all fly onto the top of his Beagle Scout hat. *Well, at least they paid attention to some of what I said,* Snoopy thinks.

It isn't long before the birds get very homesick, so Snoopy decides to cut the trip short. "It's the perfect time to head home," Snoopy tells them. They knock on Charlie Brown's door, just in time for dinner.

"Well, I guess now you probably just want to relax for a while," Charlie Brown says.

Snoopy looks at him in shock. Relax? Is he kidding? Snoopy pulls out a guitar. It's time for a little after-dinner music!

"I guess you'll never be an ordinary dog, will you, Snoopy?" Charlie Brown says. "But you know what? I don't think I'd have it any other way."

Neither would I! Snoopy thinks happily. *Neither would I!*

Go Fly a Kite, CHARLIE BROWN!

Today the sky is blue, the sun is shining, and there's a strong breeze. It's the perfect kind of day for Charlie Brown's *favorite* activity—flying a kite!

Charlie Brown arrives at an empty field—empty except for one innocent-looking tree.

He starts to run with his kite, and just as it is about to catch a gust of wind . . . he feels a sharp tug on the string.

Charlie Brown turns to see what his kite is snagged on, and finds it stuck in the tree's branches.

"Aaugh!" Charlie Brown groans. "I *knew* this was a kite-eating tree!" he shouts.

"Now, look, tree. That's my kite you've got up there, and I want it back!" he says, shaking his fist.

The tree says nothing.

"You can't argue with a kite-eating tree," Charlie Brown says to himself as he begins the sad walk home without his kite.

Charlie Brown gets to work making another kite—a red one this time.

"Back so soon?" Sally asks him.

"I'm hoping the kite-eating tree isn't in the mood for strawberry flavor," Charlie Brown replies as he heads outside with his new kite.

"Everyone likes strawberry flavor," Sally says. "Don't they?"

And sure enough, as soon as Charlie Brown starts running with the red kite . . . he feels that familiar tug on the end of the string. The tree has eaten his kite—again!

Now Charlie Brown is really angry. "If you don't let go of that kite," he yells at the tree, "I'll kick you right in the stomach!"

The tree says nothing. So Charlie Brown marches over and kicks its trunk as hard as he possibly can. But the tree still doesn't give up the kite. And now Charlie Brown's foot hurts.

"These kite-eating trees have hard stomachs," he says.

Charlie Brown goes home to make even more kites: yellow, green, and orange ones.

"Why are you making so many kites?" Sally asks.

"It liked the blueberry and the strawberry, and I bet it will like the lemon flavor too," Charlie Brown replies. "But I'd really like to find a flavor it *doesn't* like."

Sally thinks for a moment, then shrugs. "Try the lime green one!"

So Charlie Brown, along with Snoopy, heads back to the field with the yellow and green kites. Snoopy flies the yellow kite while Charlie Brown flies the green kite . . . or tries to, anyway.

The tree quickly eats Charlie Brown's kite, as usual. But he is surprised to see Snoopy flying the yellow kite high up, up, up in the air.

What did you expect? thinks Snoopy. *I'm the World's Greatest Kite Flyer!*

"I guess the tree doesn't like lemon flavor after all," Charlie Brown says. "I need to take note of that."

But when Charlie Brown attempts to fly the yellow kite himself, the tree eats it. The kite-eating tree seems to eat *any* kite Charlie Brown is flying.

"I can't stand it. I just can't stand it!" Charlie Brown exclaims.

"What would you do if I decided not to fly any more kites this year?" he asks the tree. When he doesn't get a reply, he shouts, "You'd starve to death, that's what you'd do!"

Charlie Brown is still mad, but a small part of him feels better knowing that the tree needs him. *It's nice to be needed*, Charlie Brown thinks to himself.

That's when he runs into Lucy and Linus.

"You hate that tree, don't you, Charlie Brown?" asks Linus.

Charlie Brown nods. "You know why I hate it? Because it's greedy, that's why! Even while it has a kite in its branches, it'll reach out and grab another one! It's like a little kid eating french fries. One is never enough!"

Linus and Lucy decide to check out the kite-eating tree
for themselves.

"Don't get too close," warns Charlie Brown as they
walk away.

When she sees the tree, Lucy gets an idea. *If the kite-eating tree eats kites, maybe it also eats dirty blue baby blankets that certain little brothers need to stop carrying everywhere,* she thinks.

"I don't want to live in a world where kite-eating trees exist," says Linus sadly, as he looks up at the pieces of kite poking out of the tree.

That's when Lucy takes his blanket . . .

. . . and feeds it to the kite-eating tree, which gobbles it right up.

Linus stands in shock for a moment. "My own sister threw my blanket up in a kite-eating tree!" he wails, and runs to Charlie Brown and Snoopy to ask for help.

Snoopy immediately puts on his Rescue Squad hat.
"Here comes the captain of the Rescue Squad!" shouts
Charlie Brown. "He's going to save Linus's blanket!"
"That silly beagle won't be able to save anything,"
says Lucy as Snoopy starts to climb the trunk of the tree.
"Beagles can't climb trees!"

We can't? thinks Snoopy.

He continues to try to climb the tree anyway. He makes it about halfway up before he realizes Lucy is right.

Why am I doing this? he thinks as he slides to the ground with a loud *thud!*

"Now I'll never get my blanket back!" cries Linus. "Just like Charlie Brown has never gotten a kite back!"

"Stand back, everyone," Lucy says, exasperated. "I'll get your silly blanket back." Then she yells up at the kite-eating tree, "You give that blanket back right now, do you hear me? It may be babyish, but it's my brother's, and I shouldn't have let you eat it!"

The tree shudders and Linus's blanket falls out, along with several old, chewed-up kites.

"I thought I'd never see my blanket again," says Linus, hugging it close.

"Look, Charlie Brown, there's one good kite left!" Linus exclaims.

"You're right!" says Charlie Brown. "But . . . there's no more wind to fly it in."

Snoopy has an idea . . . and calls on Woodstock and the Beagle Scouts to help him with it.

"Look, Snoopy!" says Charlie Brown. "For once I got the
better of the kite-eating tree. I'm finally flying a kite!"
Snoopy raises his eyebrows.

"Sort of," Charlie Brown adds, when he realizes *how* he is flying a kite. "Good grief!"

Lose the Blanket, LINUS!

This is Linus. Linus loves his blanket more than anything in the world.

When Linus holds his blanket, he feels like everything will be all right, no matter what happens.

His sister, Lucy, however, thinks differently. His blanket annoys her. "When are you going to get rid of that silly blanket?" she asks.

"It's not silly," Linus replies. "It makes me feel happy. Maybe if you had a blanket, you wouldn't be so crabby."

"Crabby? Who's crabby?" Lucy shouts.

I guess from now on I'll keep my suggestions to myself, Linus thinks.

"THIS IS IT!" Lucy shouts. Her voice startles Linus, and he jumps. Lucy grabs his blanket and runs off.

I wonder what that was all about, Linus thinks. He shrugs and turns to pick up his blanket. But his blanket is nowhere to be found!

Linus is still frantically searching for his blanket
when Lucy returns. She has a huge grin on her face.
"I buried your blanket!" she tells him.

Linus can't believe his ears.

"You *buried* my blanket?" he yells. "You can't do that! I'll die without that blanket! I'll be like a fish out of water! Tell me where you buried it!"

Linus tells his friend Charlie Brown what happened. "She said she was going to cure me of the habit once and for all, so she buried my blanket!" Linus cries.

Linus looks around at his huge backyard. "How am I ever going to find it?" he says.

Charlie Brown decides to sleep over at Linus's house to help him get through the first night without his blanket. He pulls up a chair and watches Linus as he sleeps.

"Ohhhh . . . ," Linus moans. He tosses and turns in his sleep.

This is going to be a long night, Charlie Brown thinks.

Suddenly Linus opens his eyes. "Is it morning yet?" he asks.

"No, it's only ten o'clock," Charlie Brown replies.

"Ten o'clock?!" Linus exclaims. "This night is going to last forever! Anyway, Charlie Brown, it's nice of you to sit up with me."

Charlie Brown smiles at Linus. "This is what friends are for," he says.

"Good old Charlie Brown!" Linus says.

A little while later, Linus closes his eyes again. *Ah, that's good,* Charlie Brown thinks. *He's finally gone to sleep. Maybe if he makes it through the night without his blanket, he'll be all right.*

"WELL, HOW'S HE DOING?" Lucy's voice booms through the bedroom as she stomps in to check on Linus.

"So much for a good night's rest," Charlie Brown says.

The next day Lucy comes over to chat with Charlie Brown.

"You think I'm being mean because I buried Linus's blanket, don't you?" she asks.

Charlie Brown doesn't say anything.

"Well, I'm not!" Lucy continues. "I'm really doing him a favor! He's too weak to ever break the habit by himself. He's as weak as . . . why, he's as weak as *you* are, Charlie Brown!"

I don't think I like that comparison, Charlie Brown thinks.

Charlie Brown tries everything he can think of to help his friend. "I have a suggestion, Linus," he says. "Why don't you try a substitute? Would you like this dish towel?"

Linus does not like that idea at all. "Would you give a starving dog a rubber bone?" he asks. "No thank you!"

Charlie Brown shrugs. "I'm out of ideas," he says.

From the moment Linus wakes up the next day, he feels terrible. He goes into the kitchen and takes out a box of cereal for breakfast. He pours some milk on the flakes and takes a bite. He pushes the bowl away. *I can't even eat . . . everything tastes sour,* he thinks.

Lucy, meanwhile, feels just fine. She is relaxing, reading a book. "Please tell me where you buried it," Linus begs.

Lucy doesn't answer.

"I've just got to find that blanket, Charlie Brown," Linus says. "Lucy won't tell me where she buried it, so I've got to dig until I find it." Linus shovels as he speaks.

Charlie Brown admires Linus's determination. "Good luck!" he calls after him.

Snoopy can't understand why Linus is so upset. Finding things that are buried is easy for Snoopy! He sniffs around a little bit . . . and there it is!

"MY BLANKET!" Linus yells. "Oh, Snoopy! You found it!"
When Linus finally lets him go, Snoopy promptly goes back to his doghouse. *I've done my good deed for the day,* he thinks. *Time for a nap!*

"I hear Linus got his blanket back," Charlie Brown says to Lucy later.

Lucy frowns. "Yeah, your nosy dog found it. Oh well. I don't care anymore. I'm through trying to help people. They never appreciate it anyway."

Linus can't stop hugging his blanket. "I got it back! I can't believe it!" Linus says.

He holds it out in front of him and studies it. "It's been buried beneath the ground for days and days," he says. "It's dirty, it's ragged, it's torn, and it's even a little moldy."

Then he hugs it again. "But it's *my* blanket!" he says with a happy sigh.

"You do realize you can't hold on to your blanket forever," Lucy says. "Someday you are going to have to lose the blanket, Linus, whether you like it or not."

Linus tries to imagine being a grown-up. He pictures going to work in a suit and a tie. He knows he probably can't bring his blanket to work with him.

Linus nods. "That's very true, Lucy," he says. "I realize *someday* I'll have to give up my blanket."

He grins at Lucy. "But not today!"
Lucy rolls her eyes. "I give up!" she says.

It's Hockey Time, Franklin!

When it's cold outside and the pond is frozen solid, Franklin loves playing hockey with his pal Charlie Brown.

"Hockey is my favorite sport!" Franklin says. "But I also love baseball and football."

"What about Ping Pong?" Charlie Brown asks.

At the pond Franklin races out onto the ice. Charlie Brown follows. That's when he notices their friend Peppermint Patty.

"Can we share the ice?" Franklin asks. "It's hockey time!"

"Sorry, Franklin," Peppermint Patty responds, "but I'm practicing for the skating show."

"Isn't there room for all of us?" Charlie Brown asks.

"Sorry, Chuck, but I need a lot of space for my figure eights!" Peppermint Patty says.

Franklin and Charlie Brown walk sadly off the ice. "I was really looking forward to playing hockey today," Franklin says.

"I know where we can watch hockey," says Charlie Brown. He leads Franklin to Woodstock's birdbath.

Snoopy and Woodstock are standing atop the frozen water, facing off at the puck to start the game.

Franklin stares at them for a moment. "You live in a weird neighborhood, Charlie Brown," he says.

The boys turn to see their friend Lucy. She's watching the game too. Franklin and Charlie Brown sit in front of her.

"Hey!" Lucy yells. "How did you get better seats than me?!"

Snoopy and Woodstock really get into the game.
They play so hard, they break the birdbath and
crash to the ground!

After the game Franklin and Charlie Brown walk back to the pond, hoping they can finally play hockey. Snoopy, Woodstock, and Lucy come along too. . . .

Franklin admits, "You know, I had my doubts when I saw the birdbath, but that was the most exciting hockey game I've ever seen!"

Peppermint Patty's friend Marcie is visiting her at the pond. Marcie doesn't skate, so she is cheering for Patty safely from the snow.

"Smooth skating on that figure eight, sir!" she says to Peppermint Patty.

"Thanks, Marcie! But that was actually a figure twenty-seven!" Peppermint Patty responds.

Before Peppermint Patty can start her next maneuver, a group of older kids skate onto the ice and get in her way.

"Move it! I have to practice," Peppermint Patty says to the newcomers.

The older kids just laugh at her.

"We're not moving!" one of the older kids tells Peppermint Patty. "We're here to play hockey! There are ten of us and one of you, so get off the ice!" Peppermint Patty looks at the kids angrily.

Marcie sees what's happening and bravely charges onto the ice to help. "Don't let them push you around, sir! I'll help you!" Marcie is even worse at running on ice than she is at skating on it. She slips and falls.

"Oh great!" one of the kids says. "How are we supposed to play with this klutz in the way?"

Peppermint Patty has had it. "All right, you jokers! Stop being rude! It's unsportsmanlike!"

Franklin gets his gear on and skates out onto the ice. "What's going on here?" Franklin asks.

"We're fighting for control of the ice! Ten against one!" Peppermint Patty shouts.

"Don't forget me, sir!" Marcie adds. "Ten against *two*!"

Franklin has an idea. "How about we play for control of the ice?" he says to the older kids. "If you win, you get the pond to yourselves. If Peppermint Patty wins, you share the ice."

"A hockey game?" one of the kids asks. "Sounds good to us!"

"Good going, Franklin," Peppermint Patty complains. "I don't have a hockey team!"

Franklin smiles. "You do now!" he says.

Franklin looks to his friends. "What do you say? Are you ready to play a game? That's what we came here for, right?"

"I came here to figure skate," answers Peppermint Patty, "but now I'm in the mood to defeat those rascally rivals!" "Nice alliteration, sir!" Marcie declares.

Franklin and Peppermint Patty get their team into position. Franklin chooses Snoopy to be goalie. Snoopy puts on extra hockey pads.

"It's not how I imagined, but at least we *finally* get to play hockey!" announces Franklin.

"Not yet," says Peppermint Patty, motioning to Woodstock, who is resurfacing the ice with a tiny Zamboni.

When Woodstock is done, he carries the puck to the center of the ice where Peppermint Patty and the leader of the rival team are ready to face off. "You are going down!" the rival taunts.

Peppermint Patty responds by putting on her game face.

The puck hits the ice, and Peppermint Patty snags it with her hockey stick. Franklin joins her, and they charge toward the goal. Game on!

Patty skates circles around the other players. She passes the puck to Franklin, and he slaps it into the goal!

"Nice shot, Franklin!" Peppermint Patty shouts.

"Okay, this is getting embarrassing!" the rival center shouts.
"Let's go play football at my house, guys!"

"So you're giving up already?" Franklin asks.

"We don't give up," the angry center snarls. "We forfeit!"
The rival team skates off the ice.

"Thanks for your help, Franklin," Peppermint Patty says. "I owe you one."

"Don't mention it," Franklin says. "But I do have one request. Can we please play hockey now?"

"Sure!" Peppermint Patty says.

"Hold on," Charlie Brown interrupts. "Here comes the Zamboni again."

Franklin rolls his eyes. "Oh, good grief!"

Cool Like SNOOPY

THIS IS SNOOPY, THE COOLEST DOG IN TOWN.

Snoopy isn't the kind of "cool dog" that does neat tricks or wears funny outfits or can play a particularly good game of fetch. Snoopy is cool on a completely different level. What's so cool about Snoopy? Well . . .

Most dogs go for normal walks, but a normal walk just wouldn't be cool enough for Snoopy.

"Want to go for a walk?" Charlie Brown asks, getting Snoopy's leash. Snoopy runs over, doing his Happy Dance . . .

. . . right before jumping into his buggy!

COOL DOGS LIKE SNOOPY DON'T WALK—THEY RIDE.

Sometimes Snoopy's friends just don't understand what he's all about. That's because being cool also means being a trendsetter.

"All you ever do is lie on top of that doghouse when you should be chasing rabbits!" Frieda tells Snoopy.

Snoopy knows Frieda has it all wrong: Chasing rabbits is out . . . lying on top of doghouses is in!

Some ordinary dog things, like chasing rabbits or
fetching sticks, just aren't cool enough for Snoopy.
Though when Snoopy does find a cool new thing to do,
he always makes it look easy.

But no matter how cool Snoopy is, he's never too cool to help a friend in need. When Linus loses his blanket, Snoopy is there to save the day!

"Oh, Snoopy! You found it! You found it!" Linus cries, giving Snoopy a big hug.

SNOOPY IS SO COOL

that he doesn't care what
anyone thinks: He dances
like no one's watching!

THOUGH SOMETIMES EVEN COOL DOGS CAN HAVE MOMENTS OF DOUBT.

One hot afternoon Snoopy headed out to make an appearance at Lucy's pool party.

Just as Snoopy was about to jump in, he got a big surprise.

"Oh no you don't!" Lucy shouted. Snoopy wasn't invited to the party!

Snoopy walked away confused—he's the king of cool—he always gets invited to parties!

Snoopy went over to the ballpark the next day, thinking a game might cheer him up. After all, he's the best (and coolest) player on Charlie Brown's baseball team!

"Snoopy, this is a hard thing for me to say. I've traded you to Peppermint Patty's team," Charlie Brown said sadly.

After blowing a halfhearted raspberry at Charlie Brown, Snoopy left the field feeling more uncool than ever.

That night, as Snoopy lay awake on top of his doghouse, things just couldn't get any worse. He wasn't invited to Lucy's pool party, he was traded to another baseball team, and on top of that, Charlie Brown forgot to feed him dinner!

Snoopy wasn't used to being left out. It felt very . . . uncool. Then Snoopy's eyes went wide.

IS THIS IT? SNOOPY WONDERED.
AM I LOSING MY COOL?

But just as Snoopy began to despair, Linus came sneaking up to his doghouse!

"Psst! Wake up!" Linus whispered. "How would you like to go on a secret mission?"

This is quite flattering, Snoopy thought. *Beagles are very seldom invited on secret missions.*

They walked to Linus's house and went inside, where it was completely dark and quiet until someone shouted . . .

"SURPRISE!"

All his friends were dressed in party hats, and Linus's house was decked out with balloons and streamers.

"We're sorry about yesterday and today, Snoopy," Charlie Brown said. "We had to keep you away while we planned your surprise. We wanted to throw you a party to show how special you are to us."

As Charlie Brown served up the cake, Snoopy smiled wide and all his doubts disappeared. Only the coolest dog in town could have such an awesome party with such great friends.

Messy Like PIGPEN

MEET PIGPEN, THE MESSIEST KID AROUND.

Pigpen takes disheveled to a whole new level. He is surrounded by a cloud of dirt, jumps in every mud puddle, and refuses to take a shower! Why? Pigpen believes he's covered in the dust of ancient civilizations. "Who am I to disturb history?" he always says.

Every move Pigpen makes raises a cloud of dust:

When he claps his hands at something funny on TV, puffs of dirt completely block the screen.

When he reaches out to catch a baseball, he creates such a dust storm that he blends in with the outfield!

"Good grief!" Charlie Brown says when the dust starts to bother him. "Does messiness run in your family, Pigpen, or is your environment to blame?"

"It must be my environment. I'm covered with it!" Pigpen says.

THERE ARE SOME ADVANTAGES TO BEING MESSY:

According to Snoopy, if you put four walls around Pigpen, you would have an instant sandbox!

And when it's hot outside, the layers of
dust on Pigpen's skin keep him nice and cool.

But sometimes even Pigpen notices that all that dirt has a downside. When he plays hide-and-seek, Lucy always finds him right away! Why? Because he leaves a trail of dust behind him that leads straight to his hiding spot!

"Works every time," Lucy says.

That's when Pigpen asks her for advice.

"You're covered in dirt and dust, Pigpen," Lucy tells him. "You don't need a psychiatrist. You need an archaeologist! Try to stay clean for an hour every day."

It's good advice, but when you're a dust magnet like Pigpen, it's not easy to follow!

Pigpen does *occasionally* try to be clean.

He combs his hair when there are so many leaves stuck in it that he has to use a rake.

He wipes off his eyes when there are so many layers of grit that he can't see where he's going!

One time, though, Pigpen did the unthinkable—at least for him. It all started at school. Violet's friend Patty had just asked Pigpen why he didn't at least tie his shoelaces.

"What do you want me to be? Inconsistent?" he replied.

He had a point, but that's when the teacher announced that there was going to be a big dance at school.

Pigpen was so excited that he decided to do the one thing he disliked the most.

I THINK IT'S TIME TO TAKE A BATH, HE THOUGHT TO HIMSELF.

Pigpen scrubbed and scrubbed at the dirt with a washcloth, but it didn't work. "I think it's finally happened, Mom!" he yelled. "I've reached the point of no return!"

With a bit of elbow grease and after quite a few long, hot soaks in the tub, Pigpen was finally squeaky-clean! He headed to the dance with a spring in his step.

He was already leaving when Charlie Brown arrived and almost walked right by him.

WHO'S THE NEW KID?
CHARLIE BROWN WONDERED.

Then Charlie Brown realized the new kid was his old friend Pigpen and gasped! "Good grief, Pigpen, is that *you*? I barely recognized you!" he said.

"Neither did anyone else," Pigpen told him sadly. "They wouldn't let me in!"

"Well, at least you tried," said Charlie Brown.

While they were talking, Pigpen got more and more disheveled.

Suddenly there was a *wham*, and Pigpen was filthy again from head to toe!

"What can I say?" Pigpen said. "I'm a dust magnet!"

"You look messier than ever," Violet said when she walked by.

"Don't listen to her, Pigpen," Charlie Brown said. "I'm beginning to wonder if you really *are* carrying around the dust of an ancient civilization!"

"Sort of makes you want to treat me with more respect, doesn't it, Violet?" Pigpen said proudly.

"Thanks for standing up for me, Charlie Brown,"
Pigpen said, and pulled some candy out of his pocket.
"Here, have some gumdrops!"

Charlie Brown knew that gumdrops weren't
usually brown, but he didn't want to hurt his friend's
feelings . . . so he ate them, dirt and all!

Pigpen began to wear his grime with pride again.

HE SHOWED UP TO FRIEDA'S BIRTHDAY PARTY LOOKING DIRTIER THAN EVER.

Charlie Brown was surprised. "Aren't you worried you'll be turned away?"

Pigpen shook his head. "The present is clean!"

Sure enough, Frieda welcomed them and said, "It's wonderful to see you," as Pigpen handed the present to her.

Charlie Brown raised his eyebrows.

"Maybe the world needs messy people," Pigpen told Charlie Brown. "Otherwise the neat people would take over!"

Pigpen might be right. After all, if everything were clean and organized all the time, things might be a little *too* perfect. When you carry a cloud of dirt wherever you go, you always bring something interesting with you!

Sweet Like SALLY

CHARLIE BROWN'S SISTER, SALLY, HAS A VERY SWEET SIDE.

She's sweetest to Linus, her Sweet Babboo, but she is also helpful, kind, and forgiving—especially to herself!

What else is sweet about Sally? Well . . .

Sally lends a helping hand, even if no one asks her to. When Snoopy imagines he is in the foreign legion, he pretends to crawl across the desert in search of water. The sun beats down. Buzzards circle overhead. It all seems hopeless, until . . .

. . . Sally appears, holding his water dish.

"You looked kind of thirsty," she says, interrupting his daydream.

What's the fun in that? Snoopy pouts, but he drinks some water anyway.

Sally was only trying to help!

Sally is polite to her big brother, Charlie Brown . . . but not always for the right reasons.

"Dear brother, will you please read this book to me?" she asks in her sweetest voice. "It's for my book report."

"Sorry, Sally. You have to read it yourself," Charlie Brown says.

Sally frowns. *What's the point of asking nicely if your brother won't do your homework?*

Sally is generous with compliments . . . even if it means talking to a brick wall.

"You're a good school, you know that?" she says to the school building one day. "And you have very cute steps!"

No one has ever said that to the school before, so it starts to blush!

Sally is also really good at looking on the bright side.

"What's two times two?" Charlie Brown asks, quizzing her for a math test.

"Ten million!" Sally guesses. When her brother tells her it's the wrong answer, she still congratulates herself. "I'm getting closer," she says proudly.

Being sweet to herself is one of Sally's many life philosophies. She only chooses ones that work in her favor!

"I've developed a new philosophy, big brother," she tells Charlie Brown. "It's 'what do I care?'"

"Well, I'm very happy for you," Charlie Brown says.

"WHAT DO I CARE?" SALLY SHRUGS.

When it's time for show-and-tell at school, Sally isn't shy.

She brings her favorite person (and the sweetest kid she knows, next to Linus): herself!

When Sally wants something, she goes for it!

"I'm too busy to talk," Sally says when one of Charlie Brown's friends calls. "My brother isn't here, so I'm moving into his room."

It might not *seem* very sweet that Sally tries to take her brother's room every time he leaves town . . . but that's when her "what do I care?" philosophy comes in handy!

SALLY IS A TOUGH COOKIE,

but she has a softer side. She wears her heart on her sleeve, and her heart belongs to Linus . . . whether he likes it or not!

It all started when Sally was a baby. She crawled up to Linus and fell in love at first sight! Being a sweet baby, she did the only thing she could do. . . .

She gave Linus a kiss! But he wasn't happy about it.

Sally refused to give up. As she grew, so did her love for Linus. When they played hide-and-seek together, Sally followed her heart instead of the rules: she didn't hide at all.

Linus finished counting to ten, opened his eyes . . .

. . . and saw Sally still standing there.

"You're supposed to be hiding!" Linus said.

"I like to listen to you count, Sweet Babboo," Sally said.

"I'm not your Sweet Babboo," Linus said, and rolled his eyes.

Sally would have given anything for Linus to call her his Sweet Babbooette.

When Sally saw a football game on TV, she decided she *had* to play football with Linus! It looked like such a sweet game!

"I'll kick the ball to you," she said to Linus. "You run down the field, and I'll try to hug you."

"Tackle," Linus said. "Football players *tackle* each other."

But Sally didn't want to tackle Linus. "Hug," she said.

"TACKLE," HE CORRECTED HER.
"HUG," SHE INSISTED.

"Forget it!" Linus said, walking away.

"Stupid game!" Sally shouted, and kicked the football out of sight.

To Sally's surprise, football wasn't sweet at all.

EVEN SO, SALLY WAS STILL SWEET ON HER SWEET BABBOO, UNTIL ONE FEBRUARY MORNING.

"Sally, get up! It's time to go to school," Charlie Brown said, but she wouldn't get out of bed!

"Linus didn't send me a Valentine's Day card," she cried. "He broke my heart and I'm never going to school again! If you see my Sweet-an'-Sour Babboo, make sure he knows how mad I am!"

"Sweet-and-*Sour* Babboo? Good grief," said Charlie Brown.

A few days later, Linus got stuck in the snow and couldn't get to the bus stop. In that moment, Sally forgot that he hadn't given her a valentine or called her his Sweet Babbooette or hugged her.

Linus was, and always would be, her one and only Sweet Babboo. And she would always be his Sweet Babbooette!

CHOP
CHOP
CHOP

Sally sprang into action. "I don't care how much it costs!" she told Snoopy and Woodstock. **"BRING HIM BACK!"**

Sally's plan worked! Snoopy and Woodstock brought Linus home safely.

And finally, Sally got what she wanted. . . .

CHOP
CHOP
CHOP
CHOP

A valentine from Linus! "Here," Linus said the next day, handing it to her.

Sally stared blankly at him. He'd never been so sweet to her before. "WHAAH!" she suddenly sobbed, startling him. "Excuse me," she added, in her most polite voice. "A tear came to my eye!"

Being sweet—and courageous and determined and devoted and smart—finally paid off. Why? Because this time, Sally's sweetness really came from the heart!

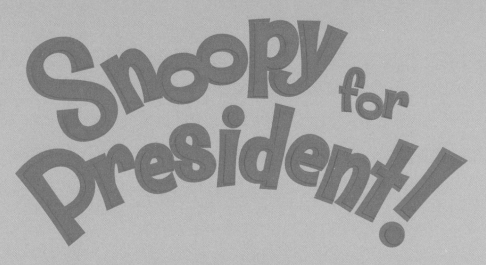

Snoopy for President!

It's a beautiful, sunny afternoon, when Snoopy hears something down below. It's Woodstock and the other birds hopping by, holding signs for different candidates for class president.

I had forgotten that this was an election year, thinks Snoopy.

One person who hasn't forgotten is Lucy. She wants her little brother Linus to become the next class president.

"But I could never be class president," says Linus. "Think of the work. Think of the responsibility."

"Think of the power," Lucy adds.

Linus smiles. Actually, that sounds pretty good. "I'll do it!" he shouts.

At school the next day Linus doesn't waste any time getting the word out.

"If I am elected class president, I will demand immediate improvements," he announces. "Any little dog who happens to wander onto the playground will *not* be chased away, but will be welcomed with open arms!"

Snoopy likes the sound of that!

But Linus has some competition. Pigpen is also running for class president, and some students are planning to vote for him. Lucy takes it upon herself to convince everyone in the school to vote for Linus.

"Hey, you!" she shouts on the playground. "Who are you gonna vote for?"

"Uh, Linus, for sure," the kid replies.

"Well, you better!" says Lucy. She turns to Linus. "According to my private poll, you now have eighty-five percent of the vote."

The next day Violet approaches Linus. She's a reporter for the school paper. "Would you care to tell us what you intend to do if you're elected class president?" she asks.

"I intend to straighten things out!" Linus says passionately. "We are in the midst of a moral decline! We are—"

Violet interrupts him. "I'll just put down that you're very honored and will do your best if elected."

"The press is against me," whines Linus as Violet walks away.

But Linus isn't done with the press. Schroeder wants to take photographs of him and Pigpen for the school paper.

"Let's pose you both with a dog," explains Schroeder.

Snoopy comes bounding out and steals the spotlight.

"Looking good, Snoopy," says Schroeder. "Maybe *you* should run for class president."

Snoopy likes the sound of that!

That afternoon Snoopy transforms his doghouse into campaign headquarters. Woodstock will be his campaign manager. He's got a lot of ideas about what Snoopy should do, but he gets so excited by them that he paces right off the doghouse!

My campaign manager isn't too bright, thinks Snoopy.

KLUNK!

CAMPAIGN HEADQUARTERS

Snoopy will just have to campaign by himself. He goes to school the next day and holds up a big sign with a paw print on it.

Lucy is not pleased. "I wouldn't vote for you if you were the last beagle on earth!" she tells him.

Snoopy starts to cry.

"All right," Lucy gives in. "If you were the last beagle on earth, I'd vote for you."

When Lucy walks away, Snoopy smiles.

Sally approaches Snoopy next. "I'm not sure if I'll vote for you or not," she says.

Once again Snoopy starts to cry.

"All right! All right!" Sally says. "I'll vote for you. Just stop crying!"

He's got a winning campaign strategy!

When Violet comes by, she asks Snoopy why she should vote for him.

When Snoopy doesn't answer, she just walks away.

But Snoopy does know the answer. *For one thing, I'm kind of groovy!* he thinks.

Not much later Lucy comes by again.

"I think you're going about this all wrong," she tells Snoopy. "You've got to do more than just carry a sign. If you're going to get elected, you're going to have to shake a lot of hands and kiss babies."

Snoopy does *not* like the sound of that!

That evening Snoopy climbs back on top of his doghouse. Tomorrow is Election Day. Each candidate for class president will give one final speech before the students vote. What will Snoopy say in his speech?

I'll tell my latest anti-cat joke, he thinks. *The dog audience will love it. But wait . . . are there any dogs at the school aside from me?*

At the assembly the next morning, Pigpen makes his speech first.

"If I'm elected class president," Pigpen begins, "I promise to—"

"You can't be class president, Pigpen," Violet yells from the audience. "You're a mess, and you have no dignity."

But Pigpen isn't discouraged. He reaches down, picks up a top hat, and puts it on. He looks just like a dusty Abe Lincoln!

Very presidential, Pigpen!

Linus goes up to the podium next. Lucy smiles. There's no way Linus can lose as long as he sticks to the script she wrote.

Linus clears his throat. "I want to talk to you this morning about the Great Pumpkin," he begins.

Everyone in the audience starts to laugh.

"AUGH!" Lucy screams.

The Great Pumpkin was the one thing Linus *wasn't* supposed to talk about. His chances of winning are over!

Snoopy is the final candidate to take the stage.
Before he goes on, Schroeder asks Snoopy what he
plans to say.

"Woof!" Snoopy replies.

"He's done for," Schroeder says to Linus.

But Snoopy is determined. He walks proudly to the podium, clears his throat, and lets out a confident bark. "Woof!"

The crowd goes wild.

A few hours later the votes are tallied. . . .

And Snoopy wins the election!

"I'm sorry you didn't get elected class president, Pigpen," says Linus.

"You too," says Pigpen. "Here we thought having photographs with a dog would get *us* votes, but instead, they all voted for the dog!"

Kick the Football, CHARLIE BROWN!

Every year when football season starts, Charlie Brown attempts to achieve one of his many goals in life: to kick a football and watch it soar through the air. And every year when Charlie Brown tries to do this, the same thing happens. It all starts with his friend Lucy.

"Over here, Charlie Brown!" says Lucy. "I've got a brand-new ball. I'll hold it, and you come running up and kick it."

Charlie Brown gets a running start and approaches Lucy. But just as he goes to kick the ball, Lucy pulls it away. Charlie Brown goes flying into the air.

"Why did you take the ball away?" Charlie Brown asks Lucy angrily.

"It suddenly occurred to me that if I let you kick it, it wouldn't be new anymore," Lucy explains.

The next time it's the same story.

"Charlie Brownnnnn!" calls Lucy in a singsong voice. "Come on. I'll hold the football, and you come running up and kick it," Lucy says. "I have a surprise for you this year."

A surprise? thinks Charlie Brown. *That must mean she isn't going to pull the football away. She's going to be surprised when she sees how far I kick that ball!*

Just like last year, Charlie Brown runs quickly at the football that Lucy's holding. Just like last year, the second he goes to kick it, Lucy pulls it away. And just like last year, Charlie Brown goes flying into the air and lands with an "AAUGH!"

"And now for the surprise," Lucy says to Charlie Brown, who can't bring himself to get up quite yet. "Would you like to see how that looked on instant replay?"

The next time Charlie Brown sees Lucy holding a football, he won't even give her a chance to talk. "No!" he shouts. "You must think I'm crazy—you say you'll hold the ball, but you won't! You'll pull it away, and I'll fall again."

"Why, Charlie Brown, I wouldn't think of such a thing," insists Lucy, smiling calmly. "I'm a changed person. Isn't this a face you can trust?"

"All right," Charlie Brown agrees begrudgingly. "You hold the ball, and I'll come running up and kick it."

This time Charlie Brown is only a little surprised when Lucy pulls away the football and he lands on his back.

"I admire you," Lucy tells him. "You have such faith in human nature."

So Charlie Brown avoids Lucy. But she knows just where to find him.

"What's up?" Sally asks when she opens the door to her house to see Lucy standing there.

"Tell your brother to come out," says Lucy. "I'll hold the ball, and he can come running up and kick it."

"She's here again," Sally says to Charlie Brown inside. "Why does she think she can fool you over and over?"

"You don't really believe my brother will fall for this, do you?" Sally asks Lucy. "I mean, after all, how often do you think you can fool someone with the same trick?"

But Charlie Brown is already following Lucy outside.

Sally stands on the front stoop and watches as Charlie Brown runs to kick the football, Lucy pulls it away, and Charlie Brown goes flying and lands on his back with an "AAUGH!"

"Pretty often, I guess," Sally remarks as Charlie Brown goes back into the house, his head spinning.

But Charlie Brown is not a quitter—and he is *not* going to give up!

"I'm going to kick that football all the way to the North Pole!" he declares.

His friends are very supportive. They believe in Charlie Brown, too! And besides, they all know how much Lucy loves her tricks . . . and they would love to see Charlie Brown get the better of her.

Linus offers to lend Charlie Brown his blanket as a good-luck charm.

Sally gives Charlie Brown a big, encouraging hug.

"Isn't this part of football, anyway?" she asks, squeezing him tight. "We're practicing right now, big brother!"

"That's tackling, not hugging," says Charlie Brown, gasping for air.

For help training, Charlie Brown turns to his most trusted friend and adviser: Snoopy.

Snoopy puts him to work, making him run laps to strengthen his legs and practice drills over and over again. He's a great coach!

After all, Snoopy's had a lot of experience with his own team.

Charlie Brown even has a dream that night that he kicks the football. And not only does he kick it, but it soars higher into the air than any football in the world! Charlie Brown knows he can do this.

The next day Charlie Brown is ready to face Lucy. And she's ready for him. She sets herself up on the grass.

"So, I'll hold the ball, Charlie Brown, and you come running—" she begins.

"Lucy!" Rerun interrupts. "Mom says to come in for lunch." Lucy ignores her little brother and turns back to Charlie Brown.

"She says right now!" shouts Rerun.

"That's all right. We'll do it some other time," says Charlie Brown.

"No, Rerun can take my place," says Lucy, handing him the football. She goes inside.

"Me?" says Rerun. He kneels on the grass and holds the football steady.

This time I'll do it! thinks Charlie Brown. *Rerun would never pull the ball away!*

"Here we go!" he shouts, gearing up to run at the ball.

A few minutes later Rerun carries the football inside to where Lucy is eating her lunch.

"What happened?" she asks. "Did you pull the ball away? Did he kick it?"

Rerun smiles mysteriously. "You'll never know."

A Best Friend for SNOOPY

Snoopy has a best friend.
His name is Woodstock.

Snoopy and Woodstock love doing everything
together—especially sharing a pizza pie!

But oh no! What's this?

Snoopy and Woodstock are reaching for the last slice of pizza—the *same* last slice of pizza. And both Snoopy and Woodstock think he should be the one to eat it!

They tug, tug, tug on the pizza slice.
They tug until it falls to the ground!

Few things can damage a friendship like a ruined slice of pizza. Snoopy thinks this is all Woodstock's fault. Snoopy tells Woodstock to go away. Snoopy walks to the far side of the doghouse. He doesn't want to listen to Woodstock's chattering anymore.

But then Snoopy realizes . . .
it's quiet.
It's too quiet.
Snoopy needs to apologize to Woodstock. But how?

Snoopy decides to get some advice from his trusty friends.
"You should buy him a blanket," Linus says.

But Snoopy doesn't think Woodstock wants a blanket.

"You need to say you're sorry in your own special way," says Charlie Brown.
Snoopy thinks this is a good idea.
He could make another pizza . . .

. . . but he doesn't have any cheese.
Snoopy does have something, though.

Lots of paint. Snoopy is an excellent painter!
He grabs some paints.
He grabs some brushes.
Snoopy gets to work!

Now all Snoopy has to do is give Woodstock
the painting.
Snoopy presents the painting to Woodstock
with a flourish!

Snoopy looks at his best friend.
Woodstock looks at him and breaks
out into a happy song!
Sharing is what best friends are for—
and Woodstock is a best friend for Snoopy!

A Best Friend for WOODSTOCK

Woodstock has a best friend.
His name is Snoopy.

Woodstock and Snoopy love doing everything together—especially sharing a pizza!

Both Woodstock and Snoopy think he
should get the last slice.
Snoopy tells Woodstock he's hungrier.
Woodstock chirps back that he's the guest!

They both tug hard on the last slice,
and they both lose their grip.
The last slice falls on the ground—
cheese side down!

Woodstock chatters angrily at Snoopy.
Snoopy asks him to leave!

Now Woodstock is alone.
He misses his friend!
He wants to let Snoopy know he is sorry.
But how?

Woodstock tries to get his friends the Beagle
Scouts to help him prepare a surprise for Snoopy.
But the Beagle Scouts are getting ready to go off
on a hiking adventure.

Woodstock has an idea!
He will write a special song and sing it to Snoopy!
Woodstock is good at singing—he is a bird, after all!

Woodstock returns to Snoopy's doghouse.
Snoopy is asleep, but Woodstock can't wait.
He stands on Snoopy's stomach and sings his song.

Snoopy loves his surprise.

Snoopy surprises Woodstock with a picture of him that he's painted.

And Snoopy has one more surprise.
He's bought a new pizza.
Now they know what to do—best friends share!

Snoopy and Woodstock's Great Adventure

This is Snoopy. And these are his friends Conrad, Olivier, Bill, Harriet, and Woodstock.

It is such a beautiful day that Snoopy, the world-famous Beagle Scout, is leading his troops out into the wilderness.

"Charlie Brown, I just saw your dog go by. Where is he going?" Lucy asks.

"He's taking his friends to Point Lobos on a photo hike," he answers.

"All right, troops," Snoopy calls out. "Let's have an equipment check. Bill, what did you bring?"

Bill chirps excitedly.

"A compass?" Snoopy says, surprised. "You think we're going to get lost? Woodstock, what did you bring?"

Woodstock holds up some rain gear.

"Rain gear? Good grief. It isn't going to rain."

Snoopy rolls his eyes as he looks at the rest of the things they brought. He tosses aside a flashlight from Olivier and a first-aid kit from Conrad. His friends are such worriers!

"All right, Harriet, how about you?" Snoopy barks.

Harriet smiles and proudly holds up a plate.

"An angel food cake with seven-minute frosting?" Snoopy says, relieved. "Well, I'm glad we have at least one sensible hiker in our group!"

Snoopy gestures to the forest ahead of them. "Now, on today's photo hike, you'll get to take some beautiful, and maybe unusual, pictures . . ."

But when Snoopy turns around, the scouts are just taking photos with each other! "Not of yourselves!" says Snoopy. He turns and leads the group onto the path with a sigh.

The hike begins! As they walk, they stop along the way to take pictures of fluffy clouds, tall trees, and oddly shaped rocks.

But as they reach some very overgrown weeds, Snoopy calls out a warning, "All right, troops. We're entering tall grass. This could mean queen snakes! We should walk single file—"

"Or . . . vertical file," Snoopy says under his breath, as the birds all perch on top of his hat.

Once they've cleared the tall grass, Snoopy lets the birds back down onto the path. Luckily they didn't run into any snakes, but now the ground is bumpy, and the scouts are getting tired. Hiking is hard work.

Olivier chirps a question.

"A walking stick?" asks Snoopy. "You're right. We all should have walking sticks."

Olivier volunteers to gather walking sticks for everyone.

But when Olivier returns with the sticks, there's just one problem: They're all bird-size!

This is not so helpful, thinks Snoopy as they continue along the trail.

"Can someone get up in a tree and try to see where we're going?" Snoopy asks a few hours later.

Bill silently wonders if his compass would have been helpful after all. It's easy to get lost in the woods.

Harriet flies up onto the brim of Snoopy's hat to get a good look around.

"Actually, Harriet, I was hoping you'd get up a little higher than that," Snoopy says sarcastically.

Still, Harriet sees the way! She chirps that they are on the right path—in fact, they're almost there!

As the friends head up the final hill, Snoopy has an idea.

"When we get to the top," Snoopy says, "we'll eat the angel food cake that Harriet brought."

Bill and Olivier chirp in agreement—they've really worked up an appetite!

But then Conrad chirps back angrily.

"What?" Snoopy cries. "Why can't we eat the cake at the top of the hill?"

Conrad chirps again.

"Because Harriet ate it at the bottom of the hill!" repeats Snoopy. "Argh!"

But Snoopy can't stay mad at Harriet for long. As they round the top of the hill, they finally arrive at Point Lobos, and the view is spectacular.

Snoopy takes a deep breath and looks out over the water. "There it is, gang—the Pacific Ocean!"

The scouts stare at the scenery for a long time, thinking about how beautiful it looks, until Snoopy encourages them to get out their cameras.

"Now I want you to take a lot of pictures of what you see. That's what we're here for," Snoopy instructs as the birds start snapping away.

The scouts notice that there are colorful flowers growing all around the cliffs.

Snoopy points out a pretty purple one. Bill tries to take a picture of it, but there's a bee near the flower. It's buzzing and flitting all around, and Bill can't get a good shot!

"Be polite," Snoopy tells Bill. "Ask the bee if he minds moving."

This time it's Bill who rolls his eyes.

As the sun sets and it begins to get dark, the world-famous Beagle Scout and his troops set up camp for the night.

Of course no campout is complete without marshmallows. Conrad gets a tree branch and begins roasting them . . . all at once!

As the scouts get ready to settle in for the night, they munch on the huge pile of marshmallows and gaze at the starry sky.

"Look, there's a full moon tonight," Snoopy points out.

The birds are suddenly nervous and start chirping to Snoopy all at once.

"No. There aren't such things as werewolves. That's just a myth," Snoopy reassures them and continues. "But you know who really comes out when the moon is full?"

"The Werebeagle!" Snoopy shouts, making a scary face.
All the birds dive into their sleeping bags for cover!
Snoopy laughs and laughs.